BE AN EFFECTIVE COMMUNICATOR

LEARNING TO LISTEN

AMY B. ROGERS

Rosen Publishing

NEW YORK

Published in 2022 by The Rosen Publishing Group, Inc.
29 East 21st Street, New York, NY 10010

Copyright © 2022 by The Rosen Publishing Group, Inc.

First Edition

Portions of this work were originally authored by Greg Roza and published as *Listen Up: Knowing When and When Not to Speak*. All new material in this edition was authored by Amy B. Rogers.

All rights reserved. No part of this book may be reproduced in any form without permission in writing from the publisher, except by a reviewer.

Cataloging-in-Publication Data

Names: Rogers, Amy B.
Title: Learning to listen / Amy B. Rogers.
Description: New York : Rosen YA, 2022. | Series: Be an effective communicator | Includes glossary and index.
Identifiers: ISBN 9781499470192 (pbk.) | ISBN 9781499470208 (library bound) | ISBN 9781499470215 (ebook)
Subjects: LCSH: Listening--Juvenile literature. | Interpersonal communication in children--Juvenile literature.
Classification: LCC BF323.L5 R647 2022 | DDC 153.6'8--dc23

Manufactured in the United States of America

Some of the images in this book illustrate individuals who are models. The depictions do not imply actual situations or events.

CPSIA Compliance Information: Batch #CWRYA22. For further information, contact Rosen Publishing, New York, New York, at 1-800-237-9932.

CONTENTS

INTRODUCTION 4

CHAPTER 1
WHY DO WE LISTEN? 7

CHAPTER 2
WHAT'S STOPPING YOU? 19

CHAPTER 3
THE WAYS WE LISTEN 31

CHAPTER 4
LISTENING TO FAMILY AND FRIENDS 43

CHAPTER 5
LISTENING AT SCHOOL AND WORK 55

GLOSSARY 70

FOR MORE INFORMATION 72

FOR FURTHER READING 74

INDEX 76

INTRODUCTION

When most people picture an effective communicator, they picture a great speaker. However, talking is only one part of communication. Another part—one that's just as important—is listening.

Communicating means exchanging thoughts, ideas, and feelings. This happens when someone shares information, often by speaking, and someone takes that information in, often by listening. Being a good communicator means putting just as much effort into listening as you do into speaking.

Most people think listening is easy. They think all it takes to be a good listener is to be quiet while someone else is talking. However, listening is a skill that takes work and practice to master. A good listener actively takes in what another person is saying instead of putting the focus on themselves. This might sound simple, but there are plenty of things that can get in the way of practicing good listening skills.

Sometimes, when someone else is speaking, we might be reminded of a similar experience we've had, or we might think we have good advice

Everyone has moments when they're not the best listener. It doesn't make you a bad person or a bad friend. It just means you have something to work on!

to give them. This can cause us to interrupt to share our thoughts in an effort to be helpful. However, it's usually more helpful to simply listen without interruption. People often just want someone they can talk to as they figure things out for themselves.

Even if we wait our turn to talk, our thoughts can sometimes get in the way of practicing good listening skills. We're often planning what we're going to say next when someone else is speaking. This means we're not really listening to what they're saying. We often do this without realizing it, and it's a common issue most people encounter from time to time. We're not trying to ignore the person who's speaking, but we still aren't actively listening to them.

How can we move past these common roadblocks to being a good listener? Learning to listen takes time and effort, but it's worth it. Most people want to be known as good listeners. It's an important part of being a good friend, student, coworker, and family member. Everyone needs people to listen to them sometimes—whether it's about stress at school or work, problems with family or friends, worries about the future, or good news they want to share. Listening is one of the ways we show people they matter to us, and that's why learning to listen is so important.

WHY DO WE LISTEN?

Listening is a valuable life skill. We often want someone to listen to us when we have something to share—from a good grade on a test to scary news about a loved one's health. Having someone to talk to—someone we know is truly listening to us—can make us feel respected and valued. However, when it seems like no one is listening, we can feel lonely, annoyed, or sad.

Listening is an important part of mental health. It can be hard to talk about our thoughts and feelings, and it can be especially hard to open up about mental health problems such as anxiety and depression. However, being able to trust

LEARNING TO LISTEN

that someone is listening can make it easier to ask for help when we're having a hard time.

Being a good listener doesn't just help the person who's doing the talking. It can help the listener too. Good listeners build stronger friendships, become better leaders, and learn new things about the world and the people around them. Although it can be hard to stop talking, turn off our own inner monologue, and focus on the person speaking, practicing good listening skills is very rewarding for many reasons.

LISTENING LETS US LEARN

At its most basic level, listening allows us to learn about the people we're communicating with. When we don't listen, we miss important information. This can have a negative impact on many areas of our lives. A daughter who doesn't hear her mother tell her what time to be home on a Friday night may end up getting grounded if she stays out later than the time her mother told her to be back. Students

WHY DO WE LISTEN?

Listening is an important part of leadership, especially at work.

likely won't pass a test if they fail to listen to their teacher during class.

Listening skills are a crucial part of the working world. An employee who doesn't listen to their boss may not receive the raise or promotion they were hoping for. Worse yet, they might lose their job altogether. Employees who listen carefully understand the results expected of them. Effective on-the-job listening helps build positive relationships that benefit coworkers, managers, clients, and customers. It also allows workers to solve problems and create a productive, respectful, and enjoyable working environment.

The things you're able to learn just by listening can help you achieve success in many different areas of life. Listening is an important part of being a student, it's essential for every career, and it allows you to build strong relationships with others.

BUILDING RELATIONSHIPS

Has anyone ever rolled their eyes or walked away when you were trying to say something? How did it make you feel? Being interrupted, being ignored, or having the feelings we're trying to share be dismissed can be upsetting. On the other hand, patiently listening to another person is perceived as a sign of respect, which helps forge lasting relationships.

Listening to your teachers at school shows them you respect them, and that leads to a better classroom environment, as well as better grades. Listening to your boss and coworkers creates an atmosphere of respect in the workplace. For example, if you listen to your boss when they're telling you important information, they might be more likely to listen to you when you share hopes or concerns with them.

Listening is also a way to show the people closest to you that you love them. Sometimes all people need to feel loved is for someone to listen to them with a concerned ear. The people who talk to us need to be confident that they won't be judged, ignored, interrupted, or given unsolicited advice. Showing respect and kindness by being a good listener is an important part of forming a bond of trust between two individuals, and trust is an essential component of any relationship, whether it's personal or professional.

Being a good listener is an important part of being a good friend.

HELPING IN HARD TIMES

It can be hard to be upset about something and to feel like we have no one to talk to. When we keep feelings such as sadness, anger, grief, and guilt bottled up inside, it makes us feel even worse. That's why opening up to a friend often makes us feel better. When we're going through hard times, we often just need someone to listen.

Some people think the best way to comfort a friend who comes to them with a problem is to try to cheer them up and get them to think positively. However, this isn't always what their friend is looking for, and what might seem like comforting words often sound hollow and cliché instead of helpful. Consider the following example of two friends talking after school:

Miguel: Is everything OK, Josh? You seem stressed.

Josh: My dad came home from work last night and said his company is going to be laying people off. He's worried that he might lose his job, and it's hard to find a new—

Miguel: You can't worry about that yet! It's going to be fine. Just try to think positively. Let's go to the mall to take your mind off of it.

Miguel thinks that by offering to take Josh's mind off of his problem and telling him to be positive, he's helping.

WHY DO WE LISTEN?

Sometimes when people are sad, they just want someone to acknowledge that what they're going through is hard. Good listeners learn to ask or pick up from social cues if someone wants advice or cheering up, and if they don't, they simply offer an understanding and nonjudgmental ear.

However, he doesn't give his friend what he really needs—someone to listen. Instead of listening, Miguel cuts Josh off and changes the subject, leaving Josh feeling like his problems don't matter to Miguel.

When people share their problems and are given responses like "Don't worry," they may feel the listener is brushing them off and doesn't want to actually hear them out. This kind of thinking and way of interacting with others, which ignores and minimizes any emotions and experiences that aren't happy and positive, is known as toxic positivity.

LEARNING TO LISTEN

CELEBRATING SUCCESSES

Just as people need to talk about their negative feelings and problems, they also need to share their positive feelings. Whether someone is talking about a good grade, landing a dream job, or getting a part in the school play, it's healthy to talk about accomplishments and good news. Good listeners enjoy the speaker's joy without interrupting or relating it to their own experiences.

In the following example, Sasha comes home from school with some news she's very proud of: She was asked to write for her school's newspaper. She runs in to tell her mother, Beth, who's a professional journalist. If Sasha's mother was a bad listener, the conversation might go like this:

Sasha: I can't believe it! They asked me to write an article for the paper!

Beth: Wow, that's great! I remember when I was in school, I was the editor of the school newspaper. Keep working on your writing skills, and I bet you could be the editor someday too.

In this example, Sasha's mom is trying to be supportive while encouraging her daughter to be the best she can be. However, she seems to have missed the point. Sasha was not looking for advice on how to become an editor, nor did she want her mom to compare their experiences. Rather, she was hoping to share some good news with someone

Good and Bad Habits

Most people want to believe they're good listeners. However, how can we be sure? The following are some bad and good listening habits. Think about them the next time you're listening to a friend or family member. Which good habits do you practice? Which ones do you want to be better at doing? Which bad habits do you see in yourself? How can you change those? Part of being a good listener is being able to identify both good and bad habits.

Bad Habits

- glancing frequently at your watch or phone while someone is talking to you
- yawning
- interrupting to ask questions
- texting, scrolling through social media, or playing with your jewelry or hair in a distracting manner
- judging speakers before they have a chance to finish speaking
- failing to verify the meaning behind a speaker's words and instead guessing at what they meant

Good Habits

- maintaining eye contact with the speaker
- nodding and making appropriate facial expressions (for example, smiling when a story is happy or looking concerned when a friend is sharing bad news)
- waiting for the speaker to pause to ask questions
- sitting or standing still
- allowing a speaker to finish talking before judging their words
- repeating what the speaker says in new words to verify the meaning

she's close to. Sometimes all we need to hear is "Great job!" to know someone is proud of us. Being a good listener means knowing when to let someone celebrate and giving them an enthusiastic partner in their happiness.

SERVING AS A SOUNDING BOARD

Speaking to a good listener often allows us to hear our thoughts spoken out loud. This gives us a chance to evaluate our thoughts and clarify what we believe. Sometimes all a speaker is looking for is someone who will give them a chance to vocalize their thoughts and come to a better understanding about how they feel. Some people refer to this as finding a "sounding board."

There are good things to be said about offering friends advice or telling them a personal story to show your understanding of what they're saying. However, listeners need to remember that a speaker isn't necessarily looking for those things. Advice and personal stories can have a negative effect on someone who just needs to talk through their problems with an understanding listener. Switching the conversation to our own thoughts can make the speaker feel less important and misunderstood. The speaker may also become even more confused about what they really feel because they weren't given a chance to talk through everything on their mind or in their heart.

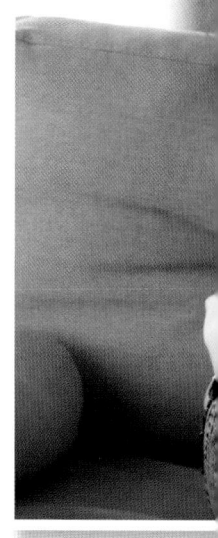

WHY DO WE LISTEN?

Good listeners understand that the person talking to them might be able to figure out how they feel simply by getting things off their chest. They know that just being there and giving someone the time and space to talk through things is often as important as—and sometimes even more valuable than—any advice they could offer.

Talking through things with a good listener can often leave you feeling better and more sure of yourself and your decisions.

A KEY TO SUCCESS

Listening is important for many different reasons. It allows us to learn, to help people, and to share in people's joy. Perhaps most importantly, listening gives us a way to show people we care about them and that they matter to us. Listening strengthens our relationships with people we love and helps us build new relationships as we go through life. It's a skill that helps us to be better workers, students, and people in general. Learning to listen is a key to becoming successful in many ways, and it starts with discovering what stands in the way of being a good listener and what we can do to overcome those obstacles.

WHAT'S STOPPING YOU?

CHAPTER 2

Think of all the sounds you hear in a day. You hear a good song in the car. You hear the sounds of lockers closing and people laughing at school. You hear the news on TV while you're eating dinner. The list goes on and on.

Sometimes we hear sounds like these and don't really pay attention to them. They're background noise while we focus on or think about something else. Unfortunately, we can sometimes treat people who are talking to us like background noise without meaning to. Hearing and listening aren't the same thing, and sometimes we miss things people tell us

LEARNING TO LISTEN

We hear a lot of sounds in a day, but we often don't really pay attention to them. However, it's important to be fully present and pay close attention when someone is speaking to you.

because we aren't using our brains to process the words other people are saying.

Why does this happen? There are many things that can stop us from being fully present in conversations and using our best listening skills. Once we recognize these obstacles, we can work to overcome them and become better listeners.

LOSING FOCUS

Has a friend ever asked for your opinion during a conversation but you couldn't answer honestly because you had been thinking about something other than their words? It happens to everyone. No matter how hard we want to listen, our minds drift. This lack of focus is one of the most common things standing in the way of good listening. Even when you have other things on your mind that you feel are important, it's necessary to put those things aside to the best of your ability when someone is talking to you.

We sometimes lose focus when other people are talking because we're already thinking about how we're going to reply. In his book *The 7 Habits of Highly Effective People*, Stephen R. Covey writes, "Most people do not listen with the intent to understand; they listen with the intent to reply." Many people are guilty of planning what they'll say when the speaker has finished talking instead of listening closely. It's natural to want to contribute to the conversation, but when we plan out what we want to say next, we aren't focusing on the speaker. It's important to remember that talking isn't the only way to contribute to a conversation. Listening has its own value and should be given the same amount of mental energy and attention.

INSECURITIES AND FEARS

Everyone has insecurities and fears. However, we can sometimes let those things get in the way of being a good listener. In some cases, a listener might feel like they're being criticized by someone who's speaking to them, whether they really are or not. Instead of carefully listening for the speaker's real meaning, they hear what they think is criticism and then respond from a defensive place. When people get defensive, they often stop listening altogether because they feel attacked.

Listening from a place of defensiveness can cause problems in our personal and professional lives. For example, during a meeting at work, Oliver's boss, Nicole, gives him some suggestions for increasing his sales. Nicole thinks Oliver is a promising salesman and wants to give him some advice to help him become the best he can be. However, Oliver feels like Nicole is criticizing his work. Oliver becomes defensive and walks out of the meeting. Not only has he missed out on an opportunity to learn from an experienced salesperson, but he's also risking his job.

Sometimes even just the fear of being criticized or seen as a failure can get in the way of being a good listener. When someone in a position of authority, such as a teacher or a boss, talks to us, we can sometimes get so wrapped up in

WHAT'S STOPPING YOU?

our assumptions and fears that they're going to criticize us or that we did something wrong that we don't pay attention to what they're saying. Fear of failure can hold us back unless we learn to relax and listen. We need to control our urge to panic when others offer suggestions for improvement. Even when we are criticized, we need to remain calm, listen, and gather as much information as we can to improve.

It can be hard to listen to a coach tell you what you need to work on. However, if you listen with an open mind instead of getting defensive and shutting them out, you can learn a lot and improve your skills.

Constructive Criticism

It doesn't always feel good to receive criticism, but learning how to listen to it, accept it, and learn from it is an important part of life. There's a difference between criticism that's unhelpful and mean and criticism that's given to help someone grow. The latter is known as constructive criticism. When people give constructive criticism, they offer specific examples of ways to improve and achievable suggestions for growth. Learning to listen to constructive criticism can help you in many aspects of your life.

A person's first instinct upon hearing any kind of criticism is often to get defensive and shut down. However, when you hear constructive criticism, it's important to be open and receptive to what the speaker is saying. Take a moment before you respond or react, because often, your first reaction will come from a place of defensiveness. Instead, listen closely to everything the speaker is saying and remember that they want to help you. Then, thank them for their suggestions, and ask questions about what they've shared. These can be questions about further ways to improve or requests for clarity or more specifics.

Constructive criticism is an important part of school, work, and even extracurricular activities such as dance classes and soccer practices. Giving it is a skill, and so is listening to it. The most important thing to remember is that it often comes from a genuine place of caring and should be listened to with respect.

JUDGMENTS AND STEREOTYPES

Another way assumptions can get in the way of listening is when we assume we know who someone is based on how they look, where they come from, or what we've been told about them by someone else. We sometimes use stereotypes to determine whether or not someone's opinion is worth listening to. In other cases, our judgments about people cause us to get defensive when listening to them just as we do when faced with the possibility of criticism. We become so sure that we know exactly what someone is going to say based on their appearance or on what someone else has told us about them that we jump to conclusions instead of listening for the truth of who they are.

When we label people rather than earnestly listening to their words, we can't possibly know who they truly are. We judge them before we really get to know them. It's only when we actually listen to others that we understand their true beliefs and intentions.

ALL ABOUT ME

When listening to others, most people naturally compare what they're hearing to their own experiences. Even when we do our best to focus on the listener's words, our brains inevitably make connections to similar situations in our own lives. Instead of keeping these thoughts to themselves, people sometimes interrupt speakers to relate their own stories. This is an example of poor listening skills in action.

LEARNING TO LISTEN

People who interrupt with these kinds of stories often have good intentions. They may want to show the speaker that they're not alone and that others have had similar experiences. The problem, however, is that the listener is presuming their experiences are the same as the speaker's experiences. This can be viewed as patronizing rather than helpful, especially when the listener tries to give advice based on their own experiences instead of seeing the speaker's story as unique.

There's a right and a wrong time to compare stories. Good listeners make a conscious effort to refrain from switching the emphasis from the speaker to themselves. Following this simple rule of listening can be difficult for some, but it's an important way to show the people in your life that you care about them and that their experiences are valid and important regardless of their connection to your own life.

UNSOLICITED ADVICE

Some listeners feel the need to offer advice, even when no one has asked for it. As in the previous example of poor listening skills, people who give unsolicited advice presume the speaker is asking for something more than just someone to listen to them.

Often, when we're thinking of what advice to give someone who's talking to us, we're not fully focused on

WHAT'S STOPPING YOU?

It can be frustrating to feel like someone is trying to fix what they think our problems are instead of actually listening.

what they're saying. We're thinking more about how we can help. While this might seem considerate, it's often not what the speaker needs. They're often looking to talk through their problems with someone who wants to listen. Trying to fix those problems for them isn't actually helpful in the long run.

FEELINGS OVER FACTS

Our emotions can also hinder our ability to listen effectively. We tend to misinterpret the words of others when we're angry, sad, and anxious. This obstacle to listening often occurs in personal relationships, such as between friends, boyfriends and girlfriends, and husbands and wives. These are the people who often bring out our strongest emotions, and problems can arise when we listen with our feelings.

In the following example, Riley and Angela have been best friends for 10 years. In high school, Riley meets a girl named Mary with whom she enjoys going to see the latest superhero movies. Riley doesn't invite Angela to go with them because she knows Angela doesn't like those kinds of movies. Angela soon becomes sad and jealous. She feels like Riley is dumping her for a new friend. Angela suggests that she tag along with them to see the latest movie, but Riley says, "I don't think you'd have fun." However, because Angela's feelings were hurt, she didn't listen to what Riley was actually saying and instead interpreted her words as, "I don't think we'd have fun with you." This interpretation hurt her feelings, but if she would have really listened to Riley, she would have realized her interpretation wasn't the truth.

It can be hard to set our feelings aside and focus on what people are actually telling us. However, good listeners need to do just that to make sure they get the real meaning behind what speakers are saying.

WHAT'S STOPPING YOU?

When we feel strong feelings, such as anger or jealousy, they can keep us from listening to the people closest to us. It's important to be able to recognize when we're feeling difficult emotions so we can understand the effect they have on how we interact with others.

A LACK OF EMPATHY

What do most of these obstacles to good listening have in common? They occur when a listener puts their own needs before the needs of the speaker. One of the strongest characteristics of a good listener is the ability to empathize with others. Empathy involves being aware of and sensitive to the thoughts and feelings of another person. Listening from an empathetic place allows us to give someone who's talking to us exactly what they need—whether that's advice, cheering up, a friend to celebrate with, or a shoulder to cry on.

MYTHS and facts

MYTH
First impressions of people are often correct, and you can usually tell what someone's like before they even speak.

FACT
It's unfair to assume you know everything about a person from how they look or carry themselves. No matter how good someone thinks they are at judging people before listening to them, stereotyping people almost always results in negative outcomes. We can't possibly understand how someone feels or who they are just by looking at them. Always give people a chance to speak before deciding what you think of them.

MYTH
Interrupting a speaker is fine as long as I have something important and relevant to say.

FACT
Interrupting someone else is almost never OK. It can cause the speaker to lose their train of thought. If you do it often enough, the speaker might not want to share things with you anymore. If possible, always wait for the speaker to pause before you ask a question or make a comment. In addition, always think about your comments and questions. Are they really important, or do you just want to put the focus of the conversation on you?

MYTH
Because you shouldn't interrupt a speaker, you should always remain passive while listening. It's the speaker's job to do all the work.

FACT
Listening is an interactive process. While it's important not to interrupt a speaker, active listeners know when to provide input, whether that means asking a question, paraphrasing the speaker's words to clarify their meaning, or giving valuable advice when it's asked for.

THE WAYS WE LISTEN

CHAPTER 3

Finding a balance between extremes is an important part of many things in life, and that's certainly true when it comes to listening. Many of the previous examples of poor listening are examples of combative listening—a listening style that is overly aggressive and focused more on the listener's agenda than the speaker.

On the other hand, passive listening is also problematic. Instead of interrupting or challenging the speaker, a passive listener is often too quiet. They want to show the speaker that they think they're important, but their lack of engagement causes its own set of problems.

LEARNING TO LISTEN

In the middle of these two types of listening is active listening. Active listeners view listening as an interactive process and work hard to make a speaker feel respected and understood.

By developing a deeper understanding of all three types of listening, we can work to improve our own listening techniques and work to be more active listeners in our everyday lives.

Combative listeners turn every conversation into a contest they want to win. This isn't an effective or empathetic way to listen.

WHAT'S COMBATIVE LISTENING?

Combative listening is also called competitive or aggressive listening. Combative listeners are focused on their own agenda. Often, they don't even hear what the speaker is saying because they're planning what they're going to say next. They interrupt speakers because they can't wait to include their opinions in the conversation. Combative listeners like to be right and often get defensive.

These kinds of listeners listen just long enough to hear what they think is most important, and then they react. They turn conversations into contests and debates, which often leads to fights instead of deeper understanding. When there are two combative listeners participating in the same conversation, it's rare that anyone else gets to speak.

WHAT'S PASSIVE LISTENING?

Unlike combative listeners, passive listeners don't want to "win" a conversation or make it all about them. Passive listeners are usually interested in what others have to say. They put so much emphasis on the speaker, though, that they rarely contribute to the conversation or offer feedback. They seldom ask questions to clarify what others say. Often, they don't say a word while speakers wait for them to respond.

While combative listeners tend to put their needs before the needs of others, passive listeners often seem meek and submissive. They rarely offer their own opinions, even when asked to do so. In some cases, passive listeners don't fully

LEARNING TO LISTEN

understand what's being said to them or asked of them because they're not actively engaged in the conversation. They can miss things because their mind wanders after listening quietly for so long.

Asking questions after a speaker is finished is an important part of listening, but passive listeners often refrain from doing this—even if it means they don't have all the information they need to succeed.

Personality Types and Listening Skills

One way to look at people's unique personalities is in terms of introversion and extroversion. These are two ends of a spectrum that describe how people get energy and interact with the world around them. More introverted people need plenty of alone time to recharge, and they often think through things carefully before speaking. On the other hand, more extroverted people get energy from interacting with the world around them, especially other people, and they tend to talk through their problems to find solutions.

More introverted people are often seen as good listeners because they aren't likely to interrupt and they often spend more time listening than talking. They also give thoughtful advice and feedback. However, that doesn't mean extroverts can't be good listeners. More extroverted people often ask good clarifying questions, and their generally positive energy in social situations can make others feel more comfortable talking to them. While it might take a little extra effort for more extroverted individuals to focus on the speaker instead of planning what they want to say or interrupting to share a story, they're often happy to share the spotlight with another speaker.

It might seem as if introverts are more passive listeners and extroverts are more combative. However, the truth is that everyone is different, and everyone can learn to be an active listener. Good listening skills are important for everyone to practice, whether you think you're a more introverted person or a more extroverted one.

WHAT'S ACTIVE LISTENING?

Active listeners stand out from the other two types of listeners in several key ways. Active listeners pay close attention to the speaker without interrupting. They ask questions to help clarify the speaker's words. They paraphrase the speaker's words to verify that they truly understand the meaning behind them. They also offer feedback if and when the speaker asks them to do so. Most importantly, they approach the speaker with an open mind and do their best to empathize with them. Active listening involves many important skills and techniques, and each one deserves special attention.

STAYING FOCUSED

When someone is speaking, active listeners concentrate on the person's words. They don't think about what they want to say next or what type of advice they should give. They avoid getting defensive, and they try to discern the real meaning behind what's being said.

Active listeners keep their mind focused on the speaker by keeping distractions such as cell phones out of reach and thoughtfully taking in each word on its own merit without jumping to conclusions or looking for comparisons to their own lives. They also keep the focus of the conversation on the speaker by avoiding interruptions. Interrupting a speaker can cause them to lose their train of thought. It can also be seen as rude.

In addition, active listeners don't rush a speaker to finish making their point. They allow speakers to gather their thoughts and express themselves at their own pace. Active listeners use quick verbal responses (such as "Go on" or "Yes") to encourage the speaker to continue without interrupting the flow of their words. This shows the speaker they are paying attention without shifting the focus to themselves.

NONVERBAL FEEDBACK

There are many nonverbal signs active listeners give to show speakers they're listening. Nonverbal communication, or body language, includes facial expressions, gestures, and other ways of showing our thoughts and feelings without words.

Active listeners know that facial expressions are an important part of showing a speaker that they're taking in what's being said. When someone is describing happy news, a smile can make that speaker feel like their joy is being shared. When someone is talking about a hard time they're going through, though, it's generally not the time to smile. Making appropriate, sincere facial expressions is a good way to show a speaker what you're feeling without interrupting them. In addition, nodding along with the speaker conveys interest without being a distraction.

The way you position your body—your posture—when others are talking also says a lot about your level of interest. For example, slouching or turning away from the speaker can make you look bored, even when you're not.

LEARNING TO LISTEN

> We communicate so much without even speaking. Yawning or slouching can make a speaker believe you're bored, so active listeners try to avoid those behaviors when someone is talking to them.

Eye contact is also very important during a conversation. If you're not looking at the speaker, the person is sure to think you don't care.

READING BETWEEN THE LINES

Active listeners know that, just as speakers analyze listeners' nonverbal signs, listeners often need to read between the lines to discover what a speaker really wants to say.

A speaker's words are the main focus of active listening, but a speaker's body language can tell a listener a lot about them too. A nervous speaker might have trouble sitting still or may be sweating. An angry speaker might talk very quickly or loudly. A speaker who is sad might avoid eye contact. These nonverbal signs can help observant, active listeners better understand the speaker's emotional state, which can shed light on the speaker's words and the meaning behind them.

It's important to note, though, that our interpretation of a speaker's words can be highly subjective. Active listeners need to recognize that their analysis of a situation is not necessarily the correct one. This is why focusing on a speaker's words, verifying information, and asking for clarification are such important parts of active listening. These actions allow listeners to get closer to the truth.

CLARIFYING AND VERIFYING

One way to clarify the meaning of a speaker's words is to ask questions. Oftentimes, the speaker leaves openings

LEARNING TO LISTEN

in the conversation to allow the listener to respond or ask questions. Asking questions shows the speaker that you care about what they're saying.

It's important to ask open questions to prompt the speaker to continue. One example is: "You said you feel terrible. What do you mean by that?" Avoid asking questions that make judgments, which can have a negative effect. An example of this kind of question is: "Don't you think you're being a little hard on your friend?"

Active listeners also make an effort to verify a speaker's words, ensuring they are on the same page as the speaker and getting the right information out of the conversation. One of the most effective ways of verifying a speaker's words is to paraphrase what you've heard. Take the meaning that you've gathered from the speaker's words and relay it back to them in your own words. You might say something like, "It sounds to me like you're discouraged about not making the team." It's important to simply summarize the meaning of the speaker's words as you have interpreted them instead of judging the speaker or trying to influence their way of thinking.

Verifying is beneficial for several reasons. It helps listeners make sure they heard the speaker correctly while encouraging the speaker to give more information. It allows speakers to restate themselves and clarify their thoughts. Verifying also shows the speaker that you're listening and want to hear more. This nonjudgmental process brings the listener and speaker closer to a mutual understanding.

WHAT DO THEY NEED?

Eventually, all speakers finish saying what they needed to say. What happens next? It depends on what the speaker was hoping to get by talking in the first place, which is what the listener needs to figure out. Sometimes the speaker just needs someone to talk to and isn't necessarily in need of a response. Other times, the speaker is talking to someone with the intention of getting feedback.

Feedback could come in the form of emotional support or even something as simple as nodding and saying, "I understand." It could also be advice, but remember, good listeners refrain from giving advice until the speaker asks for it. Through the process of active listening, a good listener will know how to respond to what a speaker needs.

Every conversation is different, and listeners need to rely on their interpretations, clarification, and verification to offer feedback tailored to the speaker and their needs. For example, if your friend is struggling with her parents' divorce, the only feedback she might need is for you to ask if she needs a hug and the assurance that her feelings are valid. However, if a teacher asks a question at school, they're expecting an answer. Practicing active listening skills in many different situations can help you become better at figuring out what people need just by hearing what they have to say.

LEARNING TO LISTEN

Listening to a parent often involves different feedback than listening to a friend. It's important to listen actively so you know what the speaker is hoping to get out of the conversation and so you can give honest, appropriate feedback when they're done.

LISTENING TO FAMILY AND FRIENDS

Two of the most common groups of people we're asked to listen to are our family and friends. Siblings come to us to talk about problems, parents speak to us about rules and expectations, and our friends talk to us about good news and hard times. Each situation is unique and should be treated as such, but there are some basic rules for active, empathetic listening that apply to most conversations with the people we're closest to.

The more you practice active listening, the better you'll get at it. These examples will help you remember what to do—and what not to do—as you work to put your listening skills into practice at home and with your friends.

LEARNING TO LISTEN

Practicing active listening skills with friends can help you grow even closer.

LEARNING TO LISTEN AT HOME

Everyone first learns to listen at home, or more specifically, in the environment in which they grow up. From a very early age, we're taught to listen to our parents or guardians. That's how we learn what's expected of us—what the rules are and what our punishment might be for breaking those rules. However, it's also how we learn that our parents or guardians love us and want the best for us.

It's important for children to listen actively to their parents or guardians, but it's important for adults to be active listeners at home too. Adults who are good listeners are more likely to keep discussions with their children calm and productive instead of combative. In addition, when adults apply active listening techniques at home, their kids learn how important it is to empathize with others and become good listeners themselves.

WHAT WENT WRONG?

Practicing active listening at home isn't always easy. There will be many times when a parent or guardian tells you something you don't want to hear. However, that's exactly when active listening skills are most useful. If you don't listen actively and instead listen from a defensive and combative place, that often only makes the situation worse.

For example, Arianna's friend Leah invited her to go on a spring break trip with her family to Florida. Arianna excitedly tells her father, Anthony, all about the week-long trip.

However, Anthony has some concerns, and the following conversation takes place:

Anthony: That's a long way to travel without your parents, and you'd be away from home for a long time.

Arianna: Leah's parents are coming with us. I'll be fine.

Anthony: I know Leah, but I've never met her parents. I'm not sure this is such a great idea. Maybe if—

Arianna: Dad, come on! They're great—trust me.

Anthony: Arianna, I can't let you travel across the country for a week with people I don't know.

Arianna: I can't believe this! You never let me do anything!

Anthony's concerns are valid, but Arianna refuses to hear what he has to say. Instead, she assumes that he's being overprotective and unfair. She interrupts him because she sees this conversation as a debate she has to win, so making her point is more important than hearing him out.

When Arianna assumes she's not going to get what she wants from the conversation, she gets defensive and shuts down instead of actively listening to what her father is saying. Because of her poor listening skills, she becomes angry and combative, ruining her chances of going on the trip.

LISTENING TO FAMILY AND FRIENDS

Becoming defensive and jumping to conclusions instead of listening actively and empathetically often means no one gets what they want or need from a conversation.

A BETTER APPROACH

If Arianna had practiced active listening skills when talking to her dad, the conversation may have gone more smoothly. The following might have happened instead:

Anthony: That's a long way to travel without your parents, and you'd be away from home for a long time.

Arianna: Leah's parents are coming with us. I'll be fine.

Anthony: I know Leah, but I've never met her parents. I'm not sure this is such a great idea. Maybe if I knew them better I'd feel more OK with letting you go.

Arianna: I understand you're worried about me being safe. What if you met with Leah's parents and talked to them? Maybe that could help you feel more comfortable with me going on the trip.

Anthony: That's a great idea. What's their number?

In this example, instead of getting upset with her father and reacting from a defensive place, Arianna remains calm. She doesn't interrupt her father because she knows that what he's saying is just as important as her thoughts about this topic. She empathizes with him so that she can better understand him and show that she cares about his feelings. She's aware of and recognizes his concern about her safety and offers a logical solution to the situation. This mature, active approach to listening is a much more likely path to an outcome that makes both parties happy.

AN IMPORTANT PART OF FRIENDSHIP

Our friends are often the people with whom we share the most emotional conversations. When we're upset about something, we usually turn to our friends for comfort. Likewise, when we have good news, we like to share it with our friends. We want our friends to empathize and listen to us in our time of need.

When we listen actively to our friends, they're more likely to listen actively to us in return.

Our friends expect us to listen this way too. When we fail to be good listeners with our friends, they may not stay our friends for long. Listening is an essential part of friendships, and being a good listener can make your friends feel valued, appreciated, and respected. However, listening poorly when a friend is sharing something—whether it's something happy or something sad—can make it seem like you don't really care about them, even when you do. When you practice good listening skills with your friends, you can help make bad times feel a little easier and good news feel even better.

WHAT WENT WRONG?

Just like at home, practicing active listening skills with your friends isn't always easy. This is especially true if your friend tells you something that reminds you of an experience you had or a story you want to tell. You might think telling that story in the middle of theirs will help show them you understand them, but it often has the opposite effect—it makes them feel unimportant. In this way, an attempt to connect with a friend through a shared experience can backfire because it seems like you're putting your need to share your story above their need to share theirs.

In the following example, Jason just got back from a summer at camp. He's excited to tell his friend Ryan all about the trip, especially how he hiked up a mountain. However, he doesn't get the chance to share his story:

Jason: Camp was amazing! I learned archery and went kayaking, and I even hiked a mountain trail! It was hard, but—

Ryan: Oh my gosh I know! I went hiking on vacation with my parents in California last year. It was so hot, but the view from the top was so cool. I could see all the way to the ocean!

Just as Jason was about to describe his favorite part of his summer at camp, Ryan interrupts to talk about his own experiences. Ryan fails to focus on his friend. Instead, he focuses on his inner voice and takes control of the conversation. By failing to keep the focus on Jason, Ryan makes Jason feel as if his story matters less.

A BETTER APPROACH

Instead of interrupting his friend to make his voice heard, Ryan should have let Jason continue to share his story about his experience at camp. By practicing active listening skills, such as those shown below, Ryan could do a better job of showing his friend that he's important to him:

Jason: Camp was amazing! I learned archery and went kayaking, and I even hiked a mountain trail! It was hard, but I had so much fun.

Ryan: That's great! What was the view like from the top?

Jason: It was so cool! The forest looked like it went on forever, and the sky was so blue. I took a ton of pictures. I can show them to you later if you want.

Ryan: That sounds amazing. What else did you do?

Not only does Ryan listen to Jason in this example without interrupting, but he also encourages him to continue. This is how friends use active listening to become closer and learn more about each other.

PRACTICE MAKES PERFECT

Listening to the people you love isn't always easy, and struggling with it sometimes doesn't make you a bad person. We have many distractions around us that make giving people our full attention difficult—phones, social media, stress from school and other areas of our lives, and our own inner monologue. However, when we make an effort to practice active listening in our everyday lives, we can get better at tuning out these distractions and giving the people we care about our full attention.

There are times, though, when listening to loved ones is harder than others. When you have a big test to study for, are tired or not feeling well, or have a lot on your mind, it can be harder to listen actively. In these cases, it's good to be honest and say to a loved one that it might be better to talk at a different time, rather than listening poorly to them at that moment. Taking care of yourself can help you better take care of others, and that includes listening to them.

Mental Health Matters!

Active listening can be an important tool when helping a friend who is dealing with mental health issues, such as depression or anxiety. If a friend reaches out to talk to you about their feelings and their struggles with their mental health, it's important to listen with empathy and without judgment. It often takes a lot of courage and strength for someone to reach out when they're feeling bad, and giving them your full attention and focus shows them that you care and want to help.

Asking clarifying questions is a big part of actively listening to a friend going through a hard time mentally and emotionally. These are some of the questions you can ask after you've listened to them share their struggles:

- Is there anything else you want to say about how you're feeling?
- Have you talked to anyone else about these problems?
- Would you like me to help you get help?
- Have you thought about hurting yourself?

Verifying how your friend is feeling and what they're experiencing is often helpful too. Saying things such as "So you've been having trouble sleeping because you feel anxious" can help your friend feel heard and can give you the information you need to help them.

However, it's important to know that some problems your friends share with you are too serious for you to listen to and handle on your own. It doesn't make you a bad listener to go to a trusted adult for help if you're worried about your friend's mental health—especially if they have talked about hurting themselves or others. In fact, that's an important part of active listening skills—reading between the lines to figure out what a speaker really needs.

LEARNING TO LISTEN

When you're stressed about homework, it can be hard to give your parents or friends your full attention when they want to talk. Explaining that you will be able to listen fully and for as long as they need once you finish your work is a way to show you care about them while also taking care of yourself.

LISTENING AT SCHOOL AND WORK

CHAPTER 5

Listening is a big part of building relationships, and it's also a key to succeeding at school and in your career. Unlike at home and with friends, you often can't tell a teacher or a boss that you'll listen to them later if you have too much on your mind; that's one way to get a bad grade or even fired from your job.

So, how can you put everything else aside to be an active listener at school and work? The following examples provide a blueprint for what to do and what not to do when it comes to listening in these environments. However, just as with family and friends, no two situations

LEARNING TO LISTEN

Actively listening at work can look different from actively listening at school. Practicing your listening skills can help you adapt to many different situations.

at school or work are exactly the same, and the listening skills you use should be tailored to who's speaking and what they need. Being able to actively listen in many different situations and to many different types of people is a skill that can help you in the classroom and far into your future.

LISTENING AT SCHOOL AND WORK

SUCCESSFUL LISTENING AT SCHOOL

It can be difficult to pay attention at school sometimes. The lesson might not be very interesting, which can lead you to focus on your own thoughts instead of what your teacher is saying. Distractions are everywhere—your friends around you, the sunshine outside, and even just watching the clock.

Despite the distractions, school can be a great place to practice active listening. Your teachers, counselors, and coaches are there to guide you and help you build the skills necessary to be successful. It's in your best interest to actively listen to them. The more you try to put your active listening skills to good use at school, the easier it will become to stay focused. Listening is how we learn, so there's no better place to practice listening than school!

WHAT WENT WRONG?

Sometimes, when a class or an assignment is hard, our first instinct is to get defensive or defeated. We often assume if a teacher wants to talk to us about our work, they're just going to say they're disappointed or scold us for doing poorly. This can keep us from really listening to

LEARNING TO LISTEN

It can be hard to talk to a teacher about struggles you're having in class, but it's important to remember that they're there to help you. Good teachers are often good listeners, and they're open to hearing about what you need to succeed in their class.

what they're saying and being open and receptive to help if they're offering it—and they're often willing to offer it.

In the following example, Cassie's Spanish teacher, Ms. Vargas, asks her to stay after class. Ms. Vargas tells Cassie that she's concerned because she did poorly on the latest quiz. She wants to know if there's anything wrong or if there's anything she can do to help. However, Cassie is less than receptive to that offer:

Ms. Vargas: You got a 65 on the last quiz. That's not like you. Is there anything you'd like to talk about or anything you'd like me to go over with you?

Cassie*:* No, I'm fine. I know I messed up.

Ms. Vargas: I'd like to help you bring your grade up. There's a study group meeting today after school. We're going to practice using the latest vocabulary words. Are you interested?

[Cassie shrugs her shoulders and looks down.]

Ms. Vargas: I could also give you an extra credit assignment to help make up—

Cassie: That's OK. I don't think it would help.

[Cassie's phone vibrates.]

Ms. Vargas: OK then. Maybe we'll see you at the study group later.

[Cassie starts texting on her way out of the room.]

    Ms. Vargas is taking the time to help Cassie, but she's not focusing on what her teacher is actually saying. Instead, she assumes that Ms. Vargas wanted to talk about how disappointed she was in her grades, and she enters the conversation from a defensive place. However, her teacher simply wants to help. If Cassie actively listened to what Ms. Vargas was saying, she'd know that her teacher was giving her an opportunity to improve because she cares about her and her performance in class.

A BETTER APPROACH

If Cassie had made an effort to let go of her feelings of failure, she could have approached her meeting with Ms. Vargas with a different mindset. Feeling defensive and making assumptions about other people and their true intentions can get in the way of really listening. Instead of shutting down before the conversation even began, Cassie could have tried the following approach:

Ms. Vargas: You got a 65 on the last quiz. That's not like you. Is there anything you'd like to talk about or anything you'd like me to go over with you?

Cassie: I think I really struggled with some of the new verbs we learned.

Ms. Vargas: I'd like to help you bring your grade up. There's a study group meeting today after school. We're going to practice using the latest vocabulary words, including those tricky verbs. Are you interested?

Cassie: So you're saying you'd help me raise my grade outside of class?

Active Listening and ADHD

Some people's brains work differently from others. For example, for people with attention-deficit/hyperactivity disorder (ADHD), paying attention and staying still can be more difficult than these behaviors are for people who don't have this disorder. ADHD commonly presents itself in one of three ways. The predominantly inattentive presentation is shown through an inability to focus, frequent daydreaming, and difficulty following conversations and directions. The predominantly hyperactive-impulsive presentation is commonly shown through a tendency to interrupt others, difficulty sitting still, and speaking and acting out at inappropriate times. The combined presentation is shown through equal elements of both of the previously outlined presentations.

Active listening presents challenges for everyone, but it can be especially challenging for people with ADHD. However, that doesn't mean it's impossible or that people with ADHD are bad listeners. They sometimes just have to work a little harder to focus or wait their turn while someone else is speaking. Some people with ADHD take medication to help them manage their symptoms. Others work with a therapist to identify problematic behaviors, including speaking out of turn, and apply positive behaviors, including visualizing a speaker's story to better focus on it, instead.

Having ADHD or any other mental or physical difference that makes listening more challenging does not mean you're a bad friend, student, or coworker because active listening doesn't come as easily to you. It can be helpful to tell the people around you that you have ADHD so they know what to expect when speaking with you, but it's also important to know that details about your physical and mental health are things you should only share if you feel comfortable doing so.

LEARNING TO LISTEN

Ms. Vargas: Absolutely. I could also give you an extra credit assignment to help make up for that quiz grade. If you do it, your average in my class wouldn't drop at all.

Cassie: Thanks, Ms. Vargas! I'd love to try that extra credit assignment, and I'll definitely come to the meeting today. I appreciate your help!

Instead of letting her assumption that she'd disappointed her teacher affect her attitude, Cassie focuses on Ms. Vargas and can see that she genuinely wants to help her. Being open to help rather than defensive gives Cassie an opportunity to raise her grade and understand the material better. Cassie also uses effective clarifying questions and paraphrasing to make sure she has all the information she needs. Active listening is a big part of success at school!

Listening actively at school can help you learn and make friends.

LISTENING AT SCHOOL AND WORK

10 Great Questions TO ASK A TEACHER

1. What listening skills can help me most at school?

2. How do teachers use active listening skills?

3. What does it mean to put myself in a speaker's shoes?

4. What does paraphrasing mean?

5. How do I read a person's body language when they're speaking or when they're listening to me speak?

6. Why is eye contact so important when listening to someone?

7. Why is it disrespectful to interrupt a speaker?

8. What do I do if I don't know the answer to a speaker's question?

9. How can judging a speaker before I hear what they have to say affect how I listen to them?

10. How can active listening help me in the future?

LEARNING TO LISTEN

ACTIVE LISTENING IN THE WORKPLACE

Listening to bosses and managers is not the same as listening to friends, parents, and teachers. Bosses aren't always interested in helping their workers grow and learn the way parents and teachers are, and bosses may or may not be their workers' friends. All bosses want one thing from their employees above all else—and that's for them to do their assigned job and to do it well.

Coworkers, too, are not necessarily going to be friends. This is not to say your coworkers and bosses can't be your friends, especially as you get older. In fact, work environments where everyone cares about their fellow workers are often the most productive. The bottom line, however, is that active listening looks different in the workplace than it does at school and among friends.

WHAT WENT WRONG?

Working at a job that deals with the public, such as a store or a restaurant, means coming into contact with many different people every day. This provides employees with many opportunities to practice actively listening to people to find

LISTENING AT SCHOOL AND WORK

Although the relationship between a boss and their employees is different from a friendship, a good boss still works hard to be an active listener when their employees need it. As such, successful employees show this same respect by listening intently when their boss is speaking.

out what they need instead of assuming they know before speaking with them.

For example, Alex works at a store that sells laptops and other electronics. One day, Mrs. Park, an elderly woman who lives alone, comes into the shop. Her clothes are old and worn. Alex doesn't think she can afford a new laptop—or that she'd

LEARNING TO LISTEN

even know how to use one. Instead of helping her, he'd rather help the young woman who came in at about the same time. She's wearing a nice dress and high heels; she looks like someone who could afford an expensive new laptop for work. Alex deals with the two customers very differently, and it's clear where his focus is, even while Mrs. Park is speaking to him:

Mrs. Park: Excuse me. I'm thinking about buying a new laptop, but I'm not sure what kind is best for me.

Alex [glancing past Mrs. Park to watch the young woman]: Well, ma'am, these laptops are very expensive.

Mrs. Park: I really need a new one. Would you be able to help me?

Alex: Maybe in a few minutes. I'm very busy at the moment.

[Alex rushes over to the young woman, leaving Mrs. Park on her own.]

Alex judges Mrs. Park by her age and appearance without truly listening to her. Not only is that disrespectful to Mrs. Park, but it also could cause her to leave and look for a laptop elsewhere. To make things worse, the young woman decides the laptops are too expensive for her budget. If Mrs. Park leaves, too, that would mean another lost sale—but this one would be because Alex didn't practice active listening skills.

A BETTER APPROACH

Had Alex used active listening with Mrs. Park, his afternoon might have been more productive. Consider this alternate example of how the conversation could go:

Alex: Can I help you, ma'am?

Mrs. Park: I'm thinking about buying a new laptop, but I'm not sure what kind is best for me.

Alex: What do you want to use it for?

Mrs. Park: I'd like to use it to talk to my grandkids and edit the pictures I take of them. Photography has always been one of my hobbies. *[She checks the price on a nearby display.]* I can afford this kind, but do you think it has enough storage space for me?

Alex: So storage space is more important than finding the lowest price?

Mrs. Park: Yes, exactly.

Alex: Let's look at a few machines, and we'll find the right one for you and your photos.

In this instance, Alex gives the customer a fair chance without judging her, and it results in a sale. It also makes Mrs. Park feel comfortable in the store, which could lead her to return or even tell friends to go there because of the great service she received.

OPEN EARS AND AN OPEN MIND

School and work are just two of the many places where active listening skills are important. While listening may seem like a passive activity that requires little effort, it actually takes a lot of practice and hard work to do it successfully. Being a good listener involves many things—focus, engagement, patience, and feedback. Good listeners are sincere in their desire to understand other people and are empathetic in their approach to communication. They listen not just with open ears but with an open mind as well.

Listening is a valuable part of communication. It's just as important as speaking and writing. Listening is how we learn about the people around us, and it's how we build strong, successful relationships in every aspect of our lives—academic, professional, and personal. When we learn to listen, we become more effective communicators and better people.

LISTENING AT SCHOOL AND WORK

You can practice active listening in many different situations every day!

GLOSSARY

academic Of or relating to school.

anxiety Fear or nervousness about something that might happen.

client A person who pays a professional person or organization for a service; a customer.

conscious Aware of something, such as a fact or feeling.

crucial Extremely important.

defensive Behaving in a way that shows that you feel people are criticizing you.

depression A serious mental condition in which a person feels sad and hopeless to the point that it interferes with daily life.

discern To see, recognize, or understand something.

emphasis Special attention or importance given to something.

engagement The state of being greatly interested in something.

forge To bring into existence.

insecurity The state of not feeling confident.

instinct A natural desire or tendency that makes a person want to act in a particular way.

intently Done with great concentration or attention.

monologue A long speech made by one person that prevents anyone else from talking.

nonverbal Not using words.

patronizing Showing you believe you are more intelligent or better than other people.

predominant More noticeable than other things.

refrain To stop yourself from doing something you want to do.

stereotype A fixed idea many people have about a thing or a group that may be untrue or only partly true.

subjective Based mainly on opinions or feelings rather than facts.

submissive Willing to give in to others.

therapist A person who helps others deal with emotional or mental problems by talking through those problems.

toxic positivity A mindset that excessively and ineffectively promotes a positive attitude at the expense of all other emotions and experiences.

unsolicited Not asked for.

verify To show or find out that something is correct.

FOR MORE INFORMATION

Center for Nonviolent Communication
1401 Lavaca Street #873
Austin, TX 78701
(505) 244-4041
Website: www.cnvc.org
The Center for Nonviolent Communication is a global organization that supports the learning and sharing of nonviolent communication skills, including active listening, and helps people peacefully and effectively resolve conflicts in personal, organizational, and political settings.

Children and Adults with Attention-Deficit/Hyperactivity Disorder (CHADD)
4221 Forbes Boulevard
Suite 270
Lanham, MD 20706
(301) 306-7070
Website: chadd.org
CHADD is an organization that offers support and resources for children and adults living with ADHD and their family members and friends.

Girls Inc.
120 Wall Street, 18th Floor
New York, NY 10005
(212) 509-2000
Website: girlsinc.org
Girls Inc. is devoted to the development of the next generation of female leaders, and its mission includes fostering the development of strong interpersonal communication skills in young women and giving young women mentors who will actively listen to them.

International Listening Association
Dr. Nan Johnson-Curiskis
Executive Director
943 Park Drive
Belle Plaine, MN 56011
(952) 594-5697
Website: www.listen.org
The International Listening Association is a professional organization whose members are dedicated to learning more about the impact that listening has on all human activity.

National Alliance on Mental Illness (NAMI)
4301 Wilson Boulevard
Suite 300
Arlington, VA 22203
(703) 524-7600
Website: nami.org/Home
NAMI is an organization dedicated to raising awareness about all aspects of mental health, including offering support for those living with mental illness and tools for friends and family members to listen actively to them and help them get the help they need.

National Communication Association
1765 N Street NW
Washington, DC 20036
(202) 464-4622
Website: www.natcom.org
The National Communication Association studies all forms, modes, and consequences of communication.

FOR FURTHER READING

Beck, Michelle Dakota. *Mental Health.* Broomall, PA: Mason Crest, 2020.

Bryant, Adam, and Kevin Sharer. *The CEO Test: Master the Challenges That Make or Break All Leaders.* Boston, MA: Harvard Business Review Press, 2021.

Burstein, John. *Have You Heard? Active Listening.* New York, NY: Crabtree Publishing, 2010.

Cain, Susan, Gregory Mone, and Erica Moroz. *Quiet Power: The Secret Strengths of Introverted Kids.* New York, NY: Puffin Books, 2017.

Fitzsimons, Kate. *The Teen's Guide to Social Skills: Practical Advice for Building Empathy, Self-Esteem, & Confidence.* Emeryville, CA: Rockridge Press, 2021.

Folger, Joseph P., Marshall Scott Poole, and Randall K. Stutman. *Working Through Conflict: Strategies for Relationships, Groups, and Organizations.* New York, NY: Routledge, 2021.

Ford, Jeanne Marie. *Respecting Opposing Viewpoints.* New York, NY: Cavendish Square Publishing, 2018.

Horning, Nicole. *Living with ADHD.* New York, NY: Lucent Press, 2019.

Jackson, Donna M. *Every Body's Talking: What We Say Without Words.* Minneapolis, MN: Twenty-First Century Books, 2014.

Johnson, Robin. *Above and Beyond with Communication.* New York, NY: Crabtree Publishing, 2017.

Kuromiya, Jun. *The Future of Communication.* Minneapolis, MN: Lerner Publications, 2021.

Nardo, Don. *Teen Guide to Mental Health.* San Diego, CA: ReferencePoint Press, 2020.

Randy, Charles. *Communication Skills.* Broomall, PA: Mason Crest, 2019.

Reeves, Diane Lindsey, Connie Hansen, and Ruth Bennett. *Communication*. Ann Arbor, MI: Cherry Lake Publishing, 2021.

Skeen, Michelle. *Communication Skills for Teens: How to Listen, Express & Connect for Success.* Oakland, CA: Instant Help Books, 2016.

Spilsbury, Louise. *Family Issues? Skills to Communicate.* New York, NY: Enslow Publishing, 2019.

Vengoechea, Ximena. *Listen Like You Mean It: Reclaiming the Lost Art of True Connection.* New York, NY: Penguin Random House LLC, 2021.

INDEX

A

active listening, explanation of, 32, 36–41

ADHD and active listening, 61

advice, offering, 4–5, 11, 13, 16, 17, 26–27, 29, 30, 35, 36, 41

aggressive listening, 33

anger, 12, 28, 29, 39, 46

anxiety, 7, 28, 53

appreciated, feeling, 50

B

body language, 37–39

bosses, listening to, 10–11, 55, 64, 65

bosses as friends, 64

C

celebrating success, as reason for listening, 14–16, 18

cheering someone up, 12, 13, 29

clarifying meaning, 30, 33, 35, 36, 39–40, 41, 53, 62

combative listening, 31, 32, 33, 35

communication, meaning of, 4

comparing experiences, 14, 16, 25–26, 36, 50, 51

competitive listening, 33

constructive criticism, 24

Covey, Stephen R., 21

coworkers as friends, 64

criticism, 22–23, 24, 25

D

defensiveness, 22, 23, 24, 25, 33, 36, 45, 47, 48, 57, 60

depression, 7, 53

distractions, 15, 19, 36, 37, 52, 57

E

emotions, as obstacle to listening, 28

empathy, 29, 32, 36, 43, 45, 47, 48, 49, 53, 68

empathy, lack of, as obstacle to listening, 29

engagement, 31, 34, 68

extroverts and listening, 35

eye contact, 15, 39

F

facial expressions, 15, 37

failure, fear of, 22, 23, 60

feedback, offering, 33, 35, 36, 41, 42, 68

first impressions, 30

focus/focusing, 4, 8, 19, 21–22, 25,

26, 28, 30, 31, 33, 35, 36–37, 39, 51, 53, 57, 59, 61, 62, 66, 68

focus, losing, as obstacle to listening, 21–22

friendship, listening and, 8, 11, 49–52

G

gestures, 37

grief, 12

guilt, 12

H

habits, listening, good and bad, 15

hair, playing with, 15

hearing vs. listening, 19

helping/comforting others, as reason for listening, 12–13, 18

home, listening at, 45–49

I

ignored, being, 6, 10, 11, 13

inner monologue, as distraction to listening, 8, 52

insecurities and fears, as obstacles to listening, 22–23

interrupting, 5, 10, 11, 14, 15, 25, 26, 30, 31, 33, 35, 36, 37, 46, 48, 51, 52, 61

introverts and listening, 35

J

jealousy, 28, 29

jewelry, playing with, 15

judgment/stereotypes, 11, 13, 15, 25, 30, 40, 53, 66, 68

K

kindness, 11

L

labeling people, 25

learning, as reason for listening, 8–10, 18

listening
    and friendship, 8, 11, 49–52
    good and bad habits, 15
    at home, 45–49
    myths and facts about, 30
    obstacles to, 19–29
    reasons for, 7–18
    at school, 8–10, 18, 57–62
    ways of, 31–42
    at work, 9, 10–11, 18, 64–68

love, listening as a way of showing, 11

M

mental health problems, 7, 53
  when to get help for a friend, 53
misinterpretation, 28
myths and facts about listening, 30

N

nodding, 15, 37, 41
nonverbal communication, 37–39

O

obstacles to listening, 19–29
open mind, listening with, 23, 36, 68
open questions, 40
opinions, 21, 25, 33

P

paraphrasing a speaker's words, 30, 36, 40, 62
passive listening, 30, 31, 33–34, 35
patience, 10, 68
personality types and listening skills, 35
phone/watch, glancing at, 15
posture, 37
practicing listening skills, 4, 5, 8, 35, 41, 43, 44, 45, 50, 51, 52, 56, 57, 64, 68

Q

questions, asking, 15, 24, 30, 33, 34, 35, 36, 39–40, 53, 62
  open questions, 40
  10 great questions to ask a teacher, 63

R

reasons for listening, 7–18
relationship building, as reason for listening, 10–11, 18
reply, listening with the intent to, 21
respect, 7, 10, 11, 24, 32, 50, 65, 66

S

sadness, 7, 12, 13, 28, 39, 50
school, listening at, 8–10, 18, 57–62
7 Habits of Highly Effective People, The, 21
slouching, 37, 38
smiling, 15, 37
social media, as distraction, 15, 52
sounding board, serving as a, 16–17
success, listening as a key to achieving, 10, 18, 55, 62, 65, 68

T

teachers, listening to, 10, 55, 57, 64

texting, 15

toxic positivity, 13

trust, 7, 11, 53

U

understood, feeling, 16, 32

unsolicited advice, 11, 26–27

V

valued, feeling, 7, 50

verbal cues of encouragement, 37

verifying meaning, 15, 36, 39–40, 41, 53

W

ways of listening, 31–42

work, listening at, 9, 10–11, 18, 64–68

Y

yawning, 15, 38

PHOTO CREDITS

Cover, p. 34 Rawpixel.com/Shutterstock.com; chapter backgrounds (speech bubbles) en-owai/Shutterstock.com; p. 5 Prostock-studio/Shutterstock.com; pp. 8–9, 16–17, 26–27, 64–65 fizkes/Shutterstock.com; p. 11 Novikov Alex/Shutterstock.com; p. 13 Motortion Films/Shutterstock.com; p. 20 DGLimages/Shutterstock.com; p. 23 digitalskillet/Shutterstock.com; p. 29 Ljupco Smokovski/Shutterstock.com; p. 32 yesstock/Shutterstock.com; p. 38 Lucky Business/Shutterstock.com; p. 42 LightField Studios/Shutterstock.com; pp. 44, 49, 54, 58 Monkey Business Images/Shutterstock.com; p. 47 New Africa/Shutterstock.com; pp. 56–57 Jacob Lund/Shutterstock.com; p. 62 ESB Professional/Shutterstock.com; p. 69 silverkblackstock/Shutterstock.com.

Designer: Michael Flynn; Editor: Katie Kawa